The Fight Of Fire

By: Jayden Askew

Table Of Contents

Chapter 1 - How it begins

"Beep, Beep, Beep" My alarm clock yells as I slowly wake up. I start pressing buttons on my alarm clock as I slowly open my eyes. I press a button and my alarm clock turns off, and I open my eyes. I get out of bed and look in my drawer. I see barely enough clothes for school. "MOM!" I yell "I'M OUT OF CLOTHES!" I don't hear a reply. "Mom? Dad?" I knock on my parents door and it opens. "Mom? Dad?" No reply. I hear the bus and I jump out my window and jump down the stairs.

"WAIT!" I scream as I'm running to the bus. I get in and the bus starts going. I find my friend and sit with him. "Dude you are extremely hot." He says starting to sweat. "What?" I say. "Your burning up! You should get to the nurse!" He exclaims sweating even more. We go into the school and we go to the nurse and she checks my temperature. "Oh my... This is abnormal." She says looking worried. "What do you mean?" I ask. "Its 209!" She exclaims. "WHAT?" My friend and I yell at the same time. "I feel fine." I say. "It's not infectious so I guess you can go to class since it does not hurt. But if it starts to hurt just tell me."

My friend and I walk out of the nurses office shocked and we start to go upstairs. We finally reach our classroom and we walk in. "FIRE!" I hear as everyone runs out of class. The teacher grabs the fire extinguisher and sprays it on my head. "Hey!" I scream as water starts coming down like rain from the emergency sprinklers. The water feels like acid for a minute. "Where was the fire?" I ask "On your head!" My friend says. "WHAT?" I say. My friend stares at me. "What now?" I ask. I look at my hands. "AHHHHHHHHHHHHH" I scream noticing the fire on my hands. I try and get it but a ball of pure fire shoots through the window. "at least the fire is out" I say.

We all go to lunch. "I'm a cat!" I say "Meow!" I say for a joke. "Ha ha You're not a ca-" He stops talking. I start getting smaller... "Did I just get smaller?" I ask. "No... You got fluffier!" My friend says as he starts to freak out. He shows me a mirror and it shows a cat. A black cat with green eyes, And a little white on its chin. "AHHHH" I scream "I want to be a human!" I start to grow, taller and taller. "Did it work?" I ask "Yes..." he says looking scared.

We all went home later that day. "Strange what happened today" I think "Also why are my parents not home? Maybe if I just lay down and take a nap-" I fall asleep.

Chapter 2 - Powers?

I wake up feeling a small breeze on my face. It feels a bit cold though. I get up and go turn off the fan. The fan turns off and it starts to cool down. I look at the time. 6:30 AM. “MOM!” I yell. Silence. “Your mom’s not home.” A mysterious voice says. “Who are you?” I ask turning on the light. “Don’t you recognize me?” The voice says. I turn on my light and see nothing but an empty room. The only life form is my plant and my cat.

“I don’t need lights but thanks anyway!” Says the voice coming from my cat. “YOU CAN TALK!” I scream. “Yes I can! I can also do this!” My cat says while doing a flip. “But why have you never talked before?” I ask. “I am only talking because you can hear me!” My cat says. “Anyway I need to teach you how to use your magic!” My cat says. “First up is fire! You can control fire and produce it!” He says as I look at my hands. “So I can control fire?” I ask. He looks at me with an I-Already-Told-You-Look. “Right, so how do I control it anyway?” I ask. “Well… Ummm… You… maybe…” He starts to stutter. “You don’t know?” I ask. “You’re… You… Well, I guess I should tell you the story… Maybe a backstory can help.” He starts to say “Well… You see… There are only 20 people in the world with your powers. There all around you, and some use there powers for bad. The people that have the powers always have two powers, one an unlimited power type, Like your fire, And one with a special power type, Like your shapeshifting.” He says. “What does unlimited power mean?” I ask. “Well, It’s like a power you can do a lot of stuff with, and special is something extra. You have a good special. That’s how I’m talking to you!” He says as he smiles. “So how do other people get the news?” I ask. “Well usually other people get the news by other people, but no one knew you had the powers, so they don’t care about you.” He explains.

“So should I tell people or-” I say but my cat cuts me off “No! 16 out of 20 people use it for bad! And there looking for the 20th person! The police think the good ones are bad and the bad ones are good! If you tell people then you will be arrested!” He exclaims. “So… Where are my parents?” I ask “Long gone… the bad ones took her.” He says. “Why my parents?” I ask “I think they know who you are, but I'm not sure" He says. I hear the pet door being used "Hello!" Says a mysterious voice. "Who's there!" I yell. "Just me, chad." It says. "Hey chad! Come on in!" my cat says. My door opens, and as it opens I look right at my face level, and nothings there. I look down. "What?" I say as I see a hamster trying to get all the way in. "But... I thought hamsters and cats were enemies!" I say. "Not me and Chad! We're buddies!" My cat says, which seems weird for my CAT to say. "*This is gonna be a long day...*" I thought to myself

Chapter 3 - How to use fire.

I walk outside with Chad the hamster and Draco the cat. I see a poorly made training dummy and a few birds around it. "Thank you guys" Draco says. "Your welcome!" They all say in sink. They fly off and Draco looks at me. "Try to throw fire on this dummy!" He says. "With my hands?" I ask. "Yes! Pretend you have a ball and you're holding it with both hands!" He says. I shape my hands like I'm

holding a ball. “I’m not sure this is gonna wor-” I say but Chad cuts me off “You need to believe or it won't work!” I try believing. I look at my hands and see fire. “AH!” I scream “You were so close!” Draco says.
I try again, I shape my hands and point my face towards the training dummy. I look at my hands… a fire! I try and stay calm. The fire starts to get bigger, and bigger, and bigger.

I try not to freak out. “Now, when it’s as big as your hand, you throw it!” Draco says. It gets as big as my hand, and I throw it. “Wow!” Draco and Chad says as it goes towards the training dummy. “Boom!” I hear as it catches in flames. “Whoa” I say as it turns into ashes. “Good job!” Chad and Draco say at the same time. “Yes the boy can throw a ball…” Say’s another mysterious voice.

“Who are you this time?” I say looking around. I see a crow looking down at me. “My name is Mike.” He says flying down. He starts to glow… “Boom!” He turned into human! “You can shapeshift too?!” I say. “No I can morph, which means I can turn into things I **KILL**.” Mike says. “So you killed a crow?” I say. “Yes… I like how you look kid, I think I’m gonna take your morph.” He says. “What?” I say as he jumps towards me. He starts making a purple ball. It gets bigger. He throws it at the floor below me and smoke goes everywhere. “*I can’t move…*” I think as he starts to charge something blue. The smoke goes in my eyesight and I can’t see. I’m gonna die.

The smoke clears and there's someone in front of me. "You can't hurt him Mike!" He says. "You can't control me David!" Mike says. They start battling. The guy that Mike said is David starts running extremely fast as Mike throws a whole bunch of water on David. David pull ground out of the earth and the water hits it. "Jay! Come on!" Draco says. I run inside. "We need to find a place to hide!" Chad says.

Chapter 4 - Hiding

"This way!" Draco the cat says pointing to the stairs. We all run up the stairs to the 3rd floor. "To my room!" I say running down the hall and into my room. I shut the door and lock it. I look out the window as they fight. "Get down!" Chad says. "It's alright. it's a 1 way window." I say. Looking at them fighting. "Who are those two anyway?" I ask "They're extremely strong! If David didn't come you would've died!" I see a huge tornado take David away. "DAVID HAS JUST GOT BLOWN AWAY!" I yell "We might be safe if we-" We hear the door get hit down. "WHERE ARE YOU JAY?" We hear a scream. "Everyone! Under the bed!" Chad says. "It's too small!" I say as my cat and hamster go under it. "Use your shapeshifting! Hurry!" Draco says as he goes all the way under. "Ok… I'm a cat,

I'm a cat, I'm a cat." I say. I start to shrink. "It worked" I whisper. I hear him knock on my door. "How do I walk?" I asked. I hear him knock harder on the door. "Pretend you are on 4 legs!" Chad says. He hits down my door.

I get under the bed right on time. "Where are you?" He says as he looks all around my room. He checks everywhere, every place, under every funiture in which I could hide. He checks under my bed. "Just 2 cats and a hamster." He says as he leaves the room. We wait a while. We hear a window break. I look out my 1 way window. I see him jump out. He lands on the ground and leaves. "That was terrifying" We all say. "Why did he want me?" I ask. "Well... you have one of the 4 elements, fire. If he kills you he gets your powers." Chad says. "Wait why is fire so special?" I ask.

"Well, in the old times the goddess of power created 4 main elements. Fire, Water, Earth, and Air. And there were only 3 people who got the elements. Fire was not given, so no one really knew about fire. After fire was figured out the goddess had to give it so someone. She gave it to you, except this was when you were just born. And since you've turned 12 not to long ago, you started figuring out about your power." Draco explains. "So I'm special?" I ask. "Yes" Chad says.

Chapter 5 - The Goddesses Relocation

"We need to get you into a safe place!" Draco says. "Ok?" I say. "Follow me! But be very careful!" Draco said. We all go outside and start to sneak. It didn't work. "YOU!" Says Mike. "OH NO HE FOUND YOU!" Draco says. "YOU'RE GOING TO DIE!" Mike yells running towards me. He jumps, I duck, and he hits the wall behind me. He throws the paralyze ball at my feet. "*I can't move… Again!*" I think to myself. He starts creating his water tornado he used on david. It gets huge. "AHHHH!" I scream.

"Stop" says another mysterious voice right when he's about to use his tornado. "You will not hurt my child in spirit" The voice says. "I'm sorry your majesty." Mike says. He starts to leave in a hurry like he was afraid of the voice, but he still grumbled under his voice. "It's you!" Draco says. "You're the goddess!" Something comes from the sky. It's to bright to see. "The goddess?" I ask. "Yes, It is I." The voice says.

The light starts to ware away, and within the light, is a woman. She has golden everything like golden shoes, golden pants, golden shirt, golden eyes, and golden hair. "You're the goddess?" I ask. "Yes, and I have too much faith in you for you to die" She says. "I will help you to the spot this cat was telling you about" She says. We start going. An hour later we stop. "Here." She says. "It's a hole in a mountain." I say. "Here, look inside." She says opening the hidden iron door. I go inside. "Whoa" I say as I walk around. "It's like a mansion!" I say looking around. "Yes, and you also have guards to provide safety." The goddess says. "I wish my friend had powers to, then we could be a team!" I say to myself. "Ok" She says.

A glowing ball forms in her hand and she throws it on the ground. The light shines so bright I have to close my eyes. When I open my eyes, I see my friend. A friend with no name, but something nice about him.

Chapter 6 - The Super Team

I stare at my friend in amaze. "How did I get here?" He says. "What powers did you give him?" I ask. "Powers? I don't have any powers!" He says. "Yes you do" Say's the goddess. It takes a while but he figures out he has powers. He got the power to control earth and to go really fast. "Weren't those david's powers?" I ask. "They were... until he passed." The goddess says. "There's also a training room!" Draco says. Draco comes in the room with white wings and he's holding chad with his tail. "You can fly?" I ask. "Ya! Anyway follow me!" He says. We follow him into a room with real testing dummy's. One row is straw, another is wood, another is iron, and the last one is ruby.

"Whoa!" I say. I go up to the stairs and see 2 empty rooms. "What's this?" I ask. "It's your rooms. Here have this." The goddess says handing me a small sack. "Say what you want to decorate your room and it will come out of the bag." She says giving one to my friend. "Well my work is done. Here's the keys to the house. Bye." She says vanishing. Well then. I start decorating my room. I put a bed in the corner, a t.v. at the end of my bed, and a few other things. The door opens, and my friend comes inside my room. "Jay, you wanna be a super team?" He asks. "Super team?" I question. "Ya, a team of superheroes!" He says enthusiastically. "Ok?" I say. "Let's go fight some crime!" He says. "We don't even know how to use our powers!" I say. "I'll help you guys!" Draco says. "You have a talking cat?" My friend says. "Ya, I also have a talking hamster." I say pointing to chad. "Hi!" Chad says. "Anyway let's get to that training room!" Draco says.

We walk to the training dummy room. We get there and I throw a ball of fire on one of the training dummy's made of straw. The dummy burns and another pops out. "Cool" I say. I see my cat talking to my friend, and I see him hit a straw dummy with a spike. It looks like a spike made out of dirt. My cat grows wings out of nowhere and starts coming to me. “I’m gonna show you another cool thing!” My cat says. “First you gotta make the ball and control it! You need to be the ball and control it with your hands!” I throw the ball and I use my hands. The ball stops, and my cat looks at me. “You did it! Now make it hit the dummy! Pretend it’s in your hands and throw it!” He says. I throw it and it hits the dummy. “Yes!” I say.

Chapter 7 - The Fight

“Good job! Let’s learn another move! It’s gonna be with your friend!” Draco says “With my friend?” I ask him. I see my friend coming toward me. Ok… I guess. I look at him, and he looks at me. It looks like we're both confused. We hear a loud noise and then a knock on our door. “I got it!” I said running towards the door dodging walls. I open the door and see a man. He looks worn out and really tired, Like he just ran a marathon. “Hi…” I said looking right at his eyes. I look at his clothes and on closer inspection I notice he’s poor. “Are you gonna talk?” I ask him looking back at his eyes. “H… e… l… p…” He said slowly falling to the ground. “Guys! Some guy just fell fainted!” I yell quickly. I see my friends come in the room as scared as they could be. They see the fainted guy and go to help him. “What happened?” Draco said looking at me. “I don’t know! He said help and then fainted!” I said extremely scared. The man then opens his eyes and gets up, looking at us. His eyes turn yellow. “What the…” I questioned looking at him. “DIE!” He screams in my face.

He throws me through the room and I fly outside. Landing on my face I get back up and I get my fireball ready. I see him rush out of the house through the hole he pushed me threw. I throw my fireball at him and he throws some weird dust at me. It hurts bad. I throw another fireball and keep on throwing. He throws his dust and I fall to the floor. I barely get back up and look at him. My eyes start glowing red. My fire takes over my mind, and soon enough the whole area around us has fire around it. I throw more and more and more fireballs until I'm almost dead. I fall to the ground, and with the last of my strength I try doing something, anything with my fire. It then happens. A huge tornado made of fire forms behind me and goes toward him. I see it going toward him, and I pass out without seeing the tornado hit him itself. It’s all black, nothing around, just pure nothingness.

Chapter 8- I’m Alive?

I’m surrounded in darkness and nothingness. I see something far away and it's coming closer. It gets right up to me and stares at me. I look at it and see its the goddess. “Don’t give up yet! Stay determined!” She says. “Stay determined about what-” I can see again. I’m in a hospital bed. Theres wires all on me. “You’re alive!” I look over and see draco on a chair. “I’m alive?” I say. “How did you summon that tornado? However you did it took all of your power, and that would usually kill the user! How did you do that?” He asks. “I don’t know.” It's all I can say.

Hearing that I could’ve died, and would of if I hadn't summoned that tornado, It seems... Weird. I sit up on the bed and look around. I notice the T.V. is on, and even has the volume on. A doctor walks in, and stares at me. “You’re alive!” She says with excitement. “Yes I am.” I say. She looks at the devices that are connected to me, and looks at them. “Everything is fine... How?” She says, looking extremely worried. “How did you survive that?” She asks turning off the T.V. “I’m not sure... All I saw was black and a light." I say. "Oh, well you're alright know… I think." She says. Draco and I go back home where we automatically see chad. "Jay your friends gone!" He says. "What?!" I yell. "He just vanished!" Chad says looking around. "BOOM" We hear outside, and we can now hear people screaming. We look outside to see a giant attacking the place with magic! He looks over at us and jumps at us. I dodge and I am alive, but I'm not so sure about Draco and Chad. I jump at the giant and- I get knocked down.

I wake up on the road, with cars honking at me. I get up and none of the houses are destroyed. I run to my house to find Chad, Draco, and my friend gone. "Anyone here?" I yell, but with no response. I go outside to hear a scream. "Jay!" I hear. It sounds like a boy and 2 girls. Wait a minute, these are my friends from school! "Jay, we found you!" They say. Also just to mention, my friends are Austin (male), Ariana (female), and Cimberli (female). "What is happening?" Cimberli asks. "Ya, What is happening?" Ariana says "Whatever's happening I can kill it!" Austin says. "What do you mean by what's happening?" I ask. "With the world! There's giants, people flying, people shooting stuff at us…" Ariana says "Oh… ever since I got magic powers the-" I get cut off by Austin. "YOU HAVE MAGIC POWERS?!?!" He screams. "Yes. Anyway the world is coming after me and I need to hide, because apparently my power is very important and many people want it." I say. "Can I have a magic power?" Ariana asks. "No, I can't share it, only the goddess can" I see a flying figure with wings. "Heh, here she is now!" I say looking at her. "Hello Jay, are these your friends?" She asks

Chapter 9- The Goddess Returns

"Yes" I say. "That's a goddess?" Cimberli says. "Well, not in the actual god way, but I'm the most powerful person in the world. So I'm just a goddess to many people" She says. "Ok hold it. HOW DOES EVERYONE HAVE MAGIC?" Austin says. "I don't really care" Ariana says. "Well, they've had it for many years, but if you guys know about it then there breaking the laws of magic. You see we are supposed to keep magic to ourselves and if you know about it then they broke the rules." She says. Austin and Cimberli looks confused, but Ariana, on the other hand, is actually looking like she knew what happened in my life since I had the powers. "Can I have powers to?" Ariana asks. "Actually we did just lose a few people who use magic, so I guess." She says. The goddess then creates a sphere of light and throws it into Ariana. "Yay!" She says. "I gave you the power of earth." The goddess says. "Thanks! I can't wait to use it!" Ariana says. "Check this out guys!" I say, turning into a bird. Austin and Cimberli faint. "Cool!" Ariana says. "We should probably get your friends to the hospital." The goddess says. "Right" I say.

At the hospital, Cimberli and Austin wake up and Me and Ariana try and calm them down. "Let me get this right, You both have magic, Jay had this for a while, and Ariana just now got it?" Cimberli asks. I nod my head yes. "Ok, I think I'm getting it." Austin says. We hear slamming on our door. A little kid busts in and uses magic to throw me out the window. I get up and throw a fireball at him. It hits him and he sets on fire. Ariana throws him out the window, he lands face first on the ground. My mind goes blank for a second and then I remember something… The fire tornado. I want to try it but it might kill me… Well, you only live once!

I do the same thing I did to summon the fire tornado I make fists with my hands and think of fire tornados. I open my hand and see a small ball of fire. I throw it at him. "Is that all you got? That couldn't even kill a fl-" He gets cut off by the tornado. A huge tornado comes from behind me and makes him fly away. "I WILL COME BACK FOR YOU!" He yells going into the sky.

Chapter 10- With my friends

You know that one time when you keep getting interrupted. And that moment when you do something amazing without realizing? Well, that's about to happen. I go up to the room I was in with my friends. "Sorry, I diden-" I get cut off by the wall getting kicked down. " WHAT IS UP WITH THE INTERRUPTIONS?!?!" I scream. "Are you jay?" He asks. "No..." I lie. "YES YOU ARE" He screams throwing a ball of lighting. "OW" I yell. He throws another one, and I duck. He throws a huge one and I throw a huge fireball to counteract it. It hits him back. He looks extremely mad. He shoots lightning out of his hands and hits me. I throw everything I have and hits him a little bit. He throws everything he has and I do the same. I throw a fire tornado, and the battle is over. "That was... AWESOME!" Ariana says. "That was... SCARY!" Cimberli says "That was... Exciting!" Austin says. They all have there own opinion, and I have mine. My opinion is all of theirs combined. I think it's fun from fighting, scary because I might die, and exciting because it's a huge rush. "Ya... I'm hungry." I say. "Seriously jay? What about your parents? They took them!" Draco says. "But I'm hungry..."

I moan. “Fine, but after we need to find your parents.” Draco commands. “TO PIZZA HUT!” I scream. “How are we gonna get there?” Cimberli asks. Something I didn't think about. “Well… Um…” I mumble. “TO THE BUS!” Ariana yells. “YA!” We all scream. We go down to the bus having a conversation, and we make it. “We’re here!” We all say. We get on the bus once it comes, and we start chatting. “Are your parents alright with this?” I ask them. “My parents don’t care.” Cimberli says. “My parents think I’m with your parents.” Ariana says. “My parents think I’m asleep, but I snuck out.” Austin says. “Well then.” I say. We ask the driver to stop at pizza hut and go in. “Actually something else I didn't think of… We need money.” I state. “Oh… Crap.” Austin says. “I got some money here” Ariana says pulling out a 10 dollar bill. “I got a little.” Cimberli says pulling out a 5 dollar bill. “Great! That should get us 2 whole pizzas!” I say. We sit down and ask the person for 2 pizza’s. One is a cheese pizza and the other one is a Supreme pizza. We also get drinks. I get a Mountain Dew, and Ariana gets a Pepsi, Cimberli gets a Coke, and Austin also gets a Coke. The waiter goes into the kitchen and gets us what we want. We eat slow and talk to each other, we look at our bill after the meal. It says we owe 20 dollars, and we start to freak out, we only have $15. I look at the bill then look at the waiter coming towards us. “CHEESE IT!” I yell and we all run out. The waiter chase’s us and is running faster than we are. “We gotta go faster!”

I say I remember my powers. I start thinking hard about a leopard. I am a leopard, I am a leopard, I think to myself. I start to shrink, and get fluffier. *I AM A LEOPARD*! "Get on my back!" I say barely running. "Ok!" They all say. I feel a lot of weight on my back but I bare through it. We start running faster then the waiter. I jump up onto a table where people are eating and then onto a ladder in an alley that leads up to a room. We hide in the room hoping we won't get caught and we make no noise. After a while we go outside and we don't see the waiter. "Well, well, well. What do we have here?" said a mysterious voice. "Who's there?" I respond. "You remember me don't you?" Said the voice. A crow comes down and starts to talk. "It's me." The crow says. "RUN!" I yell. He turns into a human and flies toward us. I turn into a cheetah and tell the others to jump on my back. He starts shooting balls of water and keeps almost hitting us. "Who's he?" Cimberli asks. "He's an old enemy." I exclaim, jumping through obstacles and dodging water. I see my house in the distance and I run as fast as I can to it. I jump in and shut the door, locking it, and running to the far end of my house.

Chapter 11 -Hiding… Again?

He starts trying to blow down the door. “I have an idea, but it’s dangerous.” I say. “What is it?” Ariana asks. “I go out there and fight like a man” I explain. “I can help! Remember, the goddess gave me powers to!” She says. “I wish I had powers to.” Austin says. “Same” Cimberli adds on. “You all have powers! Deep inside of you!” I say. “So I can go out and fight it to?” Cimberli asks. “Yes! But... your powers aren't useful on the battlefield.” I say. “But you can stay here and figure out his vulnerable points!” Cimberli looks happy, and so does Ariana. “What about me?” Austin asks. “You can go out there and distract him, but don’t get hit!” I say. “Alright!” Austin says. We all go outside ready for just a human but that's not what we see. We see a large monster, made out of water, attacking the entire city. He looks back and sees us, then run towards us. Before we can react he turns his hands into hammers and jumps at us with full speed. He aims the hammer at all of us and gets ready to slam it. “I can’t move!” Cimberli says. “Neither can I!” Austin says. “Me neither!” Ariana says. “Why can I move?” I ask. “I don’t know but help us!” I try and pick them up but it dosen’t work. “You guys are glued on the ground like hot glue!” I say. “Here it comes!” They all say. I look up and see the hammer, and all the sudden the world starts to slow down. He slowly swings his hammer towards us as the others slowly struggle. I look around, and think of some way to save them. “*I got it!*” I think in my mind. The world starts to go back to normal, and the guy swinging the hammer goes to normal to. I start to summon fire, and make a shield for the others. The hammer hits it then sets on fire. Going back to its original hands, and tries to stop the fire. Soon enough, his whole body sets on fire. He turns back to a human and leers at me. "**YOU IDIOT! YOU THINK YOU CAN DEFEAT ME?! YOUR WRONG AND YOU'RE ALWAYS GONNA BE WRONG!** You know, you haven't seen the goddess in a while, have you? You know why? **I KILLED HER! I AM THE NEW GOD OF THIS WORLD! I CONTROL YOU ALL AND THE ENTIRE WORLD!**" Mike says in a creepy voice. He tries hitting me but I dodge it. "RUN!" We all yell. "**COME BACK HERE YOU MORTALS!**" Mike yells as we run. I turn into a cheetah and everyone jumps on my back. I run as fast as I can. We run into the house and slam the door again. Mike busts it open, and we run upstairs. Mike follows us. With deja vu, we run upstairs into my room. "So… you guys are back from pizza hut? Well I heard banging on the door not to long ago, and I-" Draco gets cut off by me grabbing its mouth. "Shut it!" I whisper. "Why?" Draco asks. "**JAY… WHERE ARE YOU? I KILLED THE GODDESS AND FOUND YOU ONCE SO YOU CAN'T RUN OR FIGHT!**" Mike says. Looking around we all coward in fear. "Guys, this way!" I whisper going into my closet. We all go in and I shut the door. We hear Mike burst open the door with rage. "**WHERE ARE YOU?**" he yells. He checks under my bed, then my dresser, and everywhere else. Soon enough he goes to the closet. "*BOOM!"* A sound comes from downstairs. it's probably Chad he had been hiding in the laundry room downstairs the whole time. Mike starts to go to the kitchen. Why did he have to make noise? "Guys that was probably Chad, we have to come up with a plan to help him without being seen!" I tell Them. "But how will we be able to do that?" Cimberli asks. "I have a plan" I say pointing to the vent in the closet. "I have a screwdriver" I state. "I will unscrew the vents and go get chad, while you guys barricade the door. Also ariana, try and use your magic to barricade it. All of your magic." I tell them. I unscrew the vents then turn into a iguana. "Why an iguana?" Austin asks. "Don't question me!" I say, going into the vents. "*It's a bit dusty in here.*" I think to myself. I get to the kitchen and see Chad eating chips with the microwave broken. I open the vent with iguana powers and try to get Chad's attention. "Pssst. Chad! Come here!" I whisper to him. "Huh?" He says looking over at me. I turn into a bird, and I go up to chad. "Get on my back" I whisper. "Okie" He says getting on my back. Mike walks in and I lower a bit down behind a counter so he wouldn't see me. He walks toward the counter and I go behind him. Without Mike looking I fly up to the vent and go inside of it. I gust through the vents and make it back to the room. I turn back into a human and put chad down. "How's it going?" I ask them. "It worked!" Ariana says. "I used my powers to seal the door!" I look at the door and there's a whole bunch of stuff at the door, and the door is stone.

Chapter 12 - Fighting a God.

We all hear the door getting banged on, and soon enough it breaks open. "**THAT'S IT JAY! GET OVER HERE!**" Mike says jumping at me. He hits me so hard a get thrown right out my house and into the street. He grabs me by the shirt and throws me. I fly across the city bursting through building after building, until I hit the ground. I can see mike flying towards me with his fist out. I jump out of the way and he hits a brick wall. "OW! YOU SHOULDN'T HAVE DONE THAT!" He yells, finally going back to his old voice. He raises his hand behind him, and soon there's a tsunami behind him. I throws his hand at me and the tsunami comes rushing toward me, and I run as fast as possible away from it. I can feel fire coming onto my feet, and the tsunami rushing towards me. and taking out half the city with it. I feel even more fire on my feet and after a while fire is all around my body. I run as fast as non-humanly possible but it's no use. "**YOU QUIT RUNNING. FINALLY, IT'S AN EASY KILL**." Mike says. The tsunami washes over me and I feel like a million bullets are hitting me at once. "NO!" I yell from the water. "I WON'T BE SOME EASY KILL FOR YOU!" I scream jumping out of the water, and onto the road. "**OH YES YOU WILL!**" He yells using even more water attacks. "NO YOU WON'T!" I scream. I feel something burning inside of me, something strange, and there's only one way to get rid of it. My eyes turn red with anger, and my hands turn to flames. "**YES I WI- WAIT WHY ARE YOU GROWING?!?!**" He says. "I AM TIRED OF YOU!" I yell, growing extremely huge. I'm not sure how I'm growing, but I'm already accepting it. "YOU'RE NOT A GOD AT ALL! YOU'RE A DEMON, DESTROYING THIS LAND, AND I'M HERE TO STOP YOU!" I scream with all my lungs. "**TWO CAN PLAY AT THAT GAME!**" He states, growing as large as me. I drop down, sweep his leg, and he falls to the floor. He gets back up and covers himself with water. He tries punching me but I dodge. He punches me again and I fly about forty feet. I cover myself with fire and run up to him. We start fighting, dodging, and using our powers. A stream of fire comes out of my hands and burns him. A stream of water comes out of his hand and pushes me down. Before I can get up he steps on me, and starts pushing down. I grab his foot and throw him off of me. I get up and I see he's getting ready for something HUGE. "**I W-W-WILL D-D-DEFEAT Y-YOU, N-NO MATTER H-HOW HURT I AM**!" Mike screams. "Y-YOU'RE N-NOT GONNA H-H-HURT THIS T-T-TOWN ANY MORE!" I scream. I throw fireballs at him but it does nothing. "**WHILE I'M GETTING READY TO USE THIS YOU CAN'T ATTACK ME, AND I CAN USE ANOTHER POWER WHILE I'M CHARGING THIS POWER!**" He yells, throwing a ball of red into my house. It blows up, and I can clearly see blood. "My friends..." I whisper to myself. "THAT'S IT!" My eyes turn red. "YOU WANT TO KILL THIS PLACE? FINE! BUT IF YOU WANT TO KILL MY FRIENDS, THEN YOU'RE GONNA HAVE A BAD TIME!" I scream at him, my body turning completely red. "**THOSE... THOSE EYES... THE RAGE... THE VOICE CHANGE... YOUR THE CHOSEN ONE! I CAN KILL THE CHOSEN ONE!**" He yells. He gets ready to use the power he has been charging with. He shoots it at me, and with extreme reflex, I throw a stream of fire out of my hands. He throws a stream of water out of his hands but the water looks strange. It's ultimate water, and it's a move no one in the world can dodge or avoid. I throw my fire as he throws his water. I push it back but it comes close to me again. It keeps happening until something fly's up to me and helps me. It uses a stream of something to push the water back. I notice it’s on ground, but 2 pieces of the ground that fits just its feet. “I’m here to help!” It yells with a similar voice. “Ariana?” I ask. “Yep!” She says. “I’m also here!” Cimberli yells. “Same!” Austin says. Austin and Cimberli help Ariana push back the water, and we all start pushing it back. It’s working! We all push back the water and it hits Mike. Mike fly’s all the way into the ground. We all go to the hole that he’s in and look at him. He’s back to being small, and all the sudden, He vanishes. In his place turns a light, and with that light, a woman comes to it. She mumbles something with a familiar voice. She grabs the light and grows wings. She takes her coat off and she has the suit the goddess wore. “Thank you for taking care of mike.” The goddess says. “No problem, but I wouldn't of done it if it weren't for these guys.” I say pointing to my friends. “I cannot talk, I must return the world to balance.” She says, about to disappear in mid air.

Chapter 13- Back on track

"Wait, one thing!" The goddess says "I can give one of you a new power!" She continues. "It's the power of electricity!" She stops. "I WANT IT!" Everyone except me and Ariana yell. "You!" The goddess says pointing at cimberli. She throws a ball of light and cimberli absorbs it. "Bye!" The goddess says, vanishing into thin air. "I want a power!" Austin yells. "We have no time for that! We need to find Jay's parents! I'm starving!" Draco yells, coming out of my house. "Right!" I say, shaking my head. "How do we know where they went?" I ask draco. "Mike stole them, but I'm not sure where they went." Draco says. "I'm coming for you mike!" I scream. We all run around aimlessly looking for someone that might know where mike is. "AHHH!" We hear people yelling. We all run to it and see mike torturing the town. I run up to him and push him down. "Where are my parents!" I scream in Mike's face. "I don't know!" He says. "YOU'RE THE ONE WHO TOOK THEM!" I scream louder. "Fine, stop yelling in my face!" He says. "There in a spaceship headed for the sun." He says calmly. "WHAT! WHY?" I yell some more. "Because I had strict directions that if I die then it will be sent to th-" He starts to say but I cut him off. "YOU IDIOT! YOU PUT MY PARENTS IN A SHIP HEADED FOR THE SUN?" I scream in his face. "Well, I thought they were monkeys." He says with a straight face. I start burning his face until it sets completely on fire. Mike tries to fight back but it's no use, and even he knows that. I throw my fire tornado with full power, and even the small ball hurts him. The tornado comes from behind me once again and picks him up. "*Now to find my friends*" I think to myself, still mad at mike. I run towards where my friends were when I last saw them and, to my surprise, they were still there. "THAT WAS AWESOME" Austin yells. "The **JERK** put my **PARENTS** in a **SHIP** headed for **THE SUN**." I say, still really mad. "We gotta go find them!" Ariana yells. After a bit of talking and discussing, we get on a bus headed for Washington D.C. We all pile on, each of us with a backpack of food, and find a place to sit. We all sit in a private booth for 4, and wait. "I know we're gonna find your parents, but why Washington D.C?" Cimberli asks. "It's simple!" I start. "Washington D.C. is the main state that has Nasa's headquarters." "Oh." Cimberli realizes. "Still, how do we know nasa will let us up there for free?" Austin asks. "I… Well… Um…" I try to say, but come up with nothing. "We'll force them!" Ariana says. "Um, I don't think that's a good idea…" I say, looking at ariana with a crazy look. "Well, what's your bright idea einstein?" She asks sarcastically. "Maybe if we ask them kindly and tell them how many people are about to die… a few there, like, 2?" I say. "There are ONLY 2 people!" Ariana says. "Well, what are we gonna do?" I ask. Austin opens his mouth, but we hear a loud noise on the other side of the train, like something falling through the roof. “WHERE ARE YOU JAY?!” A voice asks. I look over and see a guy, with a black aura surrounding him, and he's looking at the other side of the bus. Acting quickly, all of my friends and I hid under our seat. He walks past us, and something drops off of him. I grab it, and I go back under my seat. It’s some kind of pen with a button where the back of the pen is. “WHERE IS HE?!” The guy asks again. I look at the pen. I look back up at the guy. I hear a loud, terrifying noise, and I accidentally hit the button on the pen. Something happens, and I start going up, like all gravity just stopped. The seat breaks off and I go to the top of the bus. “THERE YOU ARE” The guy screams at me. My left foot sticks to the ceiling. “I don’t have time for this.” I say, looking like I’m bored. “Ok, because YOU'RE GONNA DIE!” He screams in my face even more. His black aura surrounds him even more, and his eyes turn black with it. His black clothing helps his look of death. “Hey emo dude, can you let me down now?” I ask him. He starts looking really mad. Clearly he doesn't know there are two other people who have powers. “DID YOU JUST CALL ME EMO?” He yells in my face again. He throws a ball of pure darkness, and a stone wall comes out of nowhere. “WHAT?! They told me he was fire…” The guy mumbles to himself. “FINE! I’LL JUST ABSORB THE STONE!” The guy says again, making another dark ball. “Its not gonna kill me.” I say, looking at him. He looks away for a second and I look down and I see ariana smiling. He throws the ball of darkness and I block it with a wall of fire. “WHAT?!” He screams. “HOW DID… THERE'S SOMEONE ELSE HERE!” He screams. “I'd be lying if I said no…” I say, looking at ariana. Ariana stands up and looks at the guy. “Hi!” She says, fully happy. “ANOTHER POWER USER?!” The screaming continues. This time he spit all on the floor, and a little bit in my face. “Watch the spit…” I say, still hanging from the roof. “WHY DO YOU LOOK BORED?! AND WHY DO YOU LOOK HAPPY?!” He screams even more, pointing at me, then Ariana. “Because clearly you don't know who I am” I say looking even more bored. I know I'm not that powerful, but I'm not in the mood to fight, so maybe He'll be scared off. “Clearly you don't know who I AM!” I thought he was done screaming, but that's a dream that will never happen. “Who are you?” Ariana says, not in a sarcastic way, but in a I-want-to-actually-know way. “I AM GRAY! KING OF ALL DARKNESS!” Gray screams even more. “The color gray actually isn't dark though…” Ariana says. I grin a bit when Gray looks away, but I quickly make it go away. “She has a point.” I say. He looks at me, and I fall to the ground. “Ow.” I say in a bored voice. I get up and he looks red. “Hey, fires my job, so don't go all red on me.” I say. “THAT'S IT” He yells louder than ever. He forms a huge ball of darkness and shoots it at me. I dodge it, and I give him an oh-no-you-didn't look. He shoots another one at me, aimed right at my head. I duck, and I get ready to use something. "*BIRD!*" I think to myself, turning into a bird. I turn into a blue jay, and I fly in the air. He shoots another dark ball. I throw a ball of fire at it, and it absorbs it. It hits me, and I fall to the ground. I turn back human. "I don't have TIME FOR THIS!" Oh great, he has me screaming now to. I throw a small ball of fire. "IS THAT THE BEST YOU CAN DO?!" Gray asks me. "No, but this is." I say, a raging fire tornado coming from behind me. "No way… THE LEGENDARY TORNADO?!" He screams, looking in horror. I look behind me and see a complete massacre. Houses coming out of the ground, cellars coming with it, trees not having a chance of staying. It's a huge tornado, taking everything with it. Gray stares in horror, as the monstrosity comes closer. It zooms to gray, and it sucks him in. The tornado vanishes, with gray in it. I fall to the ground with pride, and amazement.

Chapter 14 - To Nasa!

Once again, except on a different bus, we were headed to nasa. "This is taking FOREVVERRRR" Ariana says. "We're almost there… right Jay?" Austin asks. "Well not qu-" The bus crashes. "WHAT IS OUR LUCK?!" Cimberli screams. I can tell everyone was tired and cranky, but we need to save this ship. I look out the window, and see two amazing things. “Guys check it out! An airport, and a grappling hook!” Ok, I know the grappling hook isn't really good for us right now, but I was trained to use one. “What good is a grappling hook to us?” Cimberli asks. “Well, I just like them.” I say. I run outside and grab the grappling hook. It was a grappling hook that was put on like a bracelet or a glove, and it would stick to your hand. I grabbed it, and just put it in my jacket pocket. “Jay, let's get to the airport.” Austin says. I look up at the airport, then look back at my friends. “Let’s do this!” Ariana says, looking at me. We all walk to the entrance of the airport, and we go in. “Guys, anyone got money?” I ask. “I got $15” Ariana says. “I have a $20” Austin says. “Since when do all of you have this much money? “Looting wallets” They both respond. “WHAT?! THAT'S ILLEGAL! WHY WOULD YOU DO THAT?!” I scream. “It’s not illegal if it hasn't been claimed for 78 hours.” Ariana says. “YES IT IS!” I scream. “Jay, cool it, lets just go. I have a credit card.” Austin says. I quit trying. “Ok, onwards!” I say. We walk up more to the plane area. We use all of our money (Except $10) for plane tickets. We go up to the plane area. “Security gate!” I whisper, pointing up. I still have the grappling hook, which they would never allow. “You should just throw the grappling hook away.” Cimberli says. “NO!” I scream. “Well then what are we gonna do?” Ariana asks. “I have an idea!” I say, running outside. “What are we gonna do?" Austin asks. "Just get on the plane, I've got this!" I say. I run outside. "Well, I wonder what Jay's gonna do." Austin says. "He's always unpredictable." Cimberli says. "I think I know what he's gonna do." Ariana says. They all get on the plane for Washington D.C. "Where's Jay?" Austin asks. They question each other until the plane starts to take flight. Ariana looks out the window, and sees me. "HES OUT THERE!" Ariana exclaimed. "Grappling hook, check! Grappling hook rule book... Read!" I say to myself. "Crap! I'm late!" I say as the airplane takes flight. "Let's do this!" I say, equipping the grappling hook. "Feels snug." I say. I shoot it at the plane and it stuck to it. My feet lifted off the ground as the plane went higher. "Now for the correct window..." I say, grappling to the windows. I look around, and I see Ariana in the ninth window. I grapple to it, and I guess it made a sound cause everyone was looking at me as soon as I grappled. I wave my hand at them. I pull out a paper and I put it against the window. "He has a note!" Ariana exclaims. "It says 'Hey guys, don't tell anyone I'm here, but I need someone to go to the bathroom. DON'T USE IT!' So, who wants to go to the bathroom?" Ariana says. Everyone looks at austin. "Heh" I laugh a bit. I see austin leave, He's clearly going to the bathroom. "*I don't see why I should do this. So what if they're girls?!*" Austin thinks. He goes into the bathroom and waits. *"Swoosh"* The toilet makes a sound. The water all vanishes, and he looks down. “Hi!” I say, coming out from the toilet. “AHHHHHH!” He screams. “Don’t scream!” I say. We both come out of the bathroom and into the seats. “Hey guys!” I say. “Why are you soaking wet?” Ariana asks me. “Long story, I don’t want to talk about it right now.” I say. We sit there for a while, then we land in Washington D.C. right where we need to be. “We are now arriving at Washington D.C.. Please do not leave your seat until we have completely landed.” The speaker finished. We all got off the plane at the appropriate time. “Ok, now to Nasa!” I say, looking around. “Where exactly is Nasa?” Austin asks. “How should I know?” I ask. “I’ll get a look around the place.” I say, turning into a bird. I fly up in the sky, looking around. “I don’t see Nasa, but I think I see the Washington Monument” I yell down to my friends, looking right at me. “Cool, but where's nasa?” Ariana yells back. I can barely make out who it is, but I can see a yelling motion from ariana. I look around more, and I make out a blurry silver vision. “A ROCKET!” I scream. “GUY’S! IT’S NASA!” I started flying down. still facing the direction I was going, I turn back to human. “This way for nasa!” I say. “Did you say nasa?” Some girl randomly asks me. “Yes…” I say, hesitating. “I have a bus that's going there now! If you want to come along it would be nice to have some company!” The woman says. She has blonde hair going down to the bottom of her torso, and brown eyes. She looked trustworthy, but I was not too hasty. “How much money?" I ask. "Free, since you could just be flying there." The woman says. "You're okay with me flying?" I ask. "Who cares Jay, we get a FREE bus ride!" Austin says. We come to an agreement, then get on the bus. We start driving, and we were there in no time. "That only felt like a minute!" I say. "That's because nasa is extremely close!" The women says. We all start departing, and some people get on the bus. We wave goodbye as the bus takes off. "Now, for a spaceship!" I say. "Do you even know a plan, Einstein?" Cimberli asks. "Actually, I do!" I say, turning into an andean condor. "Get on my back!" I say, leaning my back towards them. They all get on, and I fly to where the rocket is. Everyone gets off as I change back to my normal form. "We're gonna hijack a rocket!" I say. (Kids at home, please don't do this, you will be arrested faster than you can say billyjoebobjarryjerald.) "ARE YOU CRAZY?" Cimberli yells at me. "What?" I ask. "WE'RE GONNA HIJACK A ROCKET?!" Cimberli says. "With that attitude we're not."

"THIS IS INSANE"

"No, this is sparta."

"WE CAN'T DO THIS!"

"You already stole wallets didn't you?"

"STILL, STEALING A WALLET IS ONE THING, BUT HIJACKING A ROCKET IS IN AN ENTIRELY DIFFERENT CATEGORY!"

Ok, it's true that what I'm doing is crazy, but when your parentless, you go crazy. "Fine, you can stay on land, ya' land lover!" I say. "I'm calling the cops!" Cimberli says. "And that's our signal to get out of here. Everyone in!" I scream. We all get in, but then I suddenly notice something. "Who knows how to drive one of these things?" I ask. "I don't." Ariana and austin say at the same time. "Ok, then its up to me!" I say. I go to the captain's seat, and I hear sirens. "The police!" I yell. Ariana shuts the door, and austin grabs the space suits. "Come out of the ship! We have you surrounded!" We hear from outside after we put on our spacesuits. "Sorry, but no." I yell out, pressing a button. I get the microphone that goes to the ship. "Buckle your seatbelts everyone!" I say, starting the countdown. "You have ten seconds to come out of there!" The police say. "Nine!" I yell. "Eight!" Ariana screams. "Seven!" Austin yells. "Six…" Cimberli says. "Five more seconds!" The police say. "Also, turn off the engines!" I'm clearly not doing that, they should know what I'm doing. "Four!" I scream. "Three!" Austin screams. "Two!" Ariana screams. "That's it, go in there!" The police yell. I punch the launch button, and we start flying. "YAY!" I scream. We launch into space, and the new adventure begins.

Thanks for reading and buying! This was a very difficult book to make and it took 2 years to make, even though it's short. Just saying, I'm still decently young, and I will be releasing more books soon! And yes, there WILL be a part 2. Thanks for reading!

Thank you for reading my book!

I hope you liked it! Part 2 will be out soon!

Credits:
Jayden Askew
Ariana Duffy
Cimberli Stillian
Austin Neighbors

I need 50 pages… Here's a poem!

Roses are brown,
Violets are brown,

Sunflowers are brown, Wait who pooped in my garden?!

www.ingramcontent.com/pod-product-compliance
Ingram Content Group UK Ltd.
Pitfield, Milton Keynes, MK11 3LW, UK
UKHW041905190726
13854UKWH00003B/1105

9 781365 092855